"The wonderful books in the Weird series are great resources to help build young children's social skills to address and prevent bullying."

—**Trudy Ludwig,** children's advocate and best-selling author of *Confessions of a Former Bully*

"I love this series. Kids are sure to empathize with the characters and recognize their own power to stop bullying."

—**Dr. Michele Borba,** internationally recognized child expert and author of *The Big Book of Parenting Solutions*

WEIRD!

by Erin Frankel

illustrated by Paula Heaphy

free spirit
PUBLISHING®

Acknowledgments

Heartfelt thanks to Judy Galbraith, Meg Bratsch, Steven Hauge, Michelle Lee, and Margie Lisovskis at Free Spirit for their expertise, support, and dedication to making the world a better place for children. Special gratitude to Kelsey, Sofia, and Gabriela for their enthusiasm and ideas during the creation of this book. Appreciation to Naomi Drew for her helpful comments. Thanks also to Alvaro, Thomas, Ann, Paul, Ros, Beth, and all our family and friends for their creative insight and encouragement.

Library of Congress Cataloging-in-Publication Data
Frankel, Erin.
  Weird! / by Erin Frankel ; illustrated by Paula Heaphy.
    p. cm. — (Weird series ; bk. 1)
  ISBN 978-1-57542-398-2
1. Bullying—Juvenile literature. 2. Bullying in schools—Juvenile literature. 3. Individual differences in children—Juvenile literature. 4. Self-confidence in children—Juvenile literature. I. Heaphy, Paula. II. Title.
  BF637.B85F73 2012
  302.34'3—dc23
                                                                      2012006157
eBook ISBN: 978-1-57542-660-0

Reading Level Grades 2–3; Interest Level Ages 5–9;
Fountas & Pinnell Guided Reading Level M

Edited by Meg Bratsch
Cover and interior design by Michelle Lee

10 9 8 7 6 5 4 3 2 1
Printed in Hong Kong
P17200512

Free Spirit Publishing Inc.
Minneapolis, MN
(612) 338-2068
help4kids@freespirit.com
www.freespirit.com

Free Spirit offers competitive pricing.
Contact edsales@freespirit.com for pricing information on multiple quantity purchases.

For all children,
young and old,
who have been bullied.

Don't lose sight of who you are.

Know yourself.

Be yourself.

And never let anyone take
away your polka dots.

Hi. My name is **Luisa** and I have a **problem**.

There is a **girl** in my class named Sam who thinks that **everything** I do is

WEIRD!

I raise **my hand** to answer a question in **math,** and **she** says I'm WEIRD.

3

I try telling a **funny** joke
at lunch, and **she** says I'm . . .

WEIRD!

Guess I'll just be quiet.

5

I give my **mom** a kiss when she **picks** me up from school, and Sam says I'm . . .

WEIRD!

Maybe Mom can wait
for me in the car.

I say something in **Spanish** to my **dad**, and she says
I'm WEIRD.

"Hi, Dad."

Guess it's "**Hi, Dad**" from now on.

"Weird!"

I wear my **favorite** polka dot boots,
and she says I'm WEIRD.

It's strange.
I keep **changing** what I do,
but she doesn't change at all.

She still says
I'm WEIRD.

It seems like **weird** is the **only** word
she knows, and I don't know *any* words.

"Where did all your polka dots go, Luisa?"

I don't even feel like **myself** anymore.

Everyone else **misses** the way I **used to be.**
Everyone else, including **me.**

Who should I talk to?

What will I say?

What did I do to deserve this?

I wish it all would just **go away**.

"I found your boots."

After talking to Mom, I've been **thinking**. Maybe it's time for **one more**

change.

19

So I put my **favorite** polka dot **boots** back on. Only this time, before **Sam** could say anything,

I said, "Boy, it feels **great** to be back in **these** again!"

STOP BULLYING

21

I told another **funny** joke at lunch and **laughed** along with my friends. When she said **WEIRD**, I kept on laughing.

I **didn't** hide my feelings
when I got the **right** answer in math.

25

I discovered something **really amazing!**

The more I **act** like
I don't care what **she** says,
the more I really don't care.

And the more she **thinks**
I don't care,
the more she **leaves me alone**.

Now **that's** really . . .

29

I guess
I'll just be
me
from
now on!

Luisa's Notes

Boy, am I glad I got my polka dots back—and they're not *weird* at all! Here are some things I can remember so I won't lose them again:

When I feel nervous, scared, or sad, I can think positive thoughts.

Everyone has the right to feel safe and respected, including me.

I am not to blame when someone chooses to bully me.

Remember there are people who care and want to help me if I ask them to.

Don't give anyone the power to take away what makes me special.

Sam's Notes

It used to bother Luisa when I called her "weird," but now she looks happy and confident . . . which makes me feel not so *tough* anymore. Here are some things I've been thinking about:

Trying to bully someone who ignores me isn't any fun.

Owning up to my behavior is going to be hard, but maybe it's worth it.

Until Luisa acted confident, I felt like I had power over her.

Guess bullying won't get me what I want after all.

Hearing others stand up for Luisa made me step back and think about what I was doing.

Jayla's Notes

I'm so glad Luisa is back to being herself. Now I know that I can *dare* to stand up for someone who is being bullied. Here are some other things I've learned as a bystander to bullying:

Doing what's right can be hard at first, but it always feels good in the long run.

Asking others for help makes a big difference.

Real friendship is about standing up for each other.

Encouraging Luisa to be confident in herself helped Sam stop bullying her.

Join Luisa's Confidence Club!

Acting confident isn't always easy. But the more you practice, the better you'll get. I found out that I can make some really simple changes to look, sound, and feel more confident. I can . . .

Stand up tall with my shoulders back and my head held high.

Look others in the eye—*not* down at the floor.

Speak clearly so people can understand me.

Smile and laugh if I want to!

Turn and walk away calmly when I don't like what is happening.

Tell an adult if I or someone else needs help.*

Confident means believing in yourself and your abilities.

*Telling vs. Tattling

Nobody wants to be a tattletale. But tattling on a person for something small (like picking her nose!) is very *different* from telling an adult when someone needs help. If you were being bullied, you'd want someone to help you, right?

While I am doing all this on the *outside*, I am also making changes on the *inside*. Instead of thinking negative thoughts that make me feel nervous inside, I think positive thoughts that make me feel calm and confident. Here's what I think inside my head when Sam is around:

"I am going to walk by and choose not to listen to what she is saying."

"I am *not* going to let her ruin my day."

"I am calm and confident."

"I don't have to worry about what she thinks."

"Many people like me just the way I am."

"I can always ask for help if I need it."

Can you think of other ways to look and feel confident? Share them with your friends and classmates!

Confidence Club: Recycle Your Thoughts

Help me recycle my negative thoughts into positive ones. It's easier than you think!

1. Cut out eight circles from a sheet of paper. These are your polka dots.

2. Find four of my negative thoughts in the book and write them on four of the polka dots.

3. For each negative thought, think of a positive thought to write on the other four polka dots. Then, color and decorate the *positive* polka dots.

4. Now, crinkle up the negative polka dots and toss them in the recycling bin.

5. Let's put my recycled thoughts to good use! Decorate your room with the positive polka dots. Make a mobile or a card for someone.

Next, try recycling your *own* negative thoughts into positive thoughts. With a little practice, you'll be thinking positively in no time!

Confidence Club: Step in the Right Direction

At first, I was nervous about putting my polka dot boots back on. I wondered what Sam would say when I walked by her. But when I focused on walking *away* from Sam and *toward* people who care about me, it wasn't as hard to step in the right direction!

You never know when someone might need *your* help to step in the right direction. Why not make your own poster to show you care?

1. Write "Step in the Right Direction" at the top of a poster board.

2. Trace each of your feet twice on the poster board. Draw a picture of yourself next to the last footprint.

3. Write, draw, or paste caring messages inside your footprints. You can use some of the caring messages I got in this book if you'd like.

4. Give the poster to a friend to show her or him how to step *away* from someone who is being mean and *toward* someone who cares—you!

Can you think of more fun activities we can do in our Confidence Club? Share them with your classmates and friends.

"Love those polka dots!"

"I miss your funny jokes."

"It's not your fault."

"You are wonderful just the way you are."

A Note to Parents, Teachers, and Other Caring Adults

Every day, millions of children are subjected to bullying in the form of name-calling, threats, insults, belittling, taunting, rumors, and racist slurs—and still more are witnesses to it. Verbal bullying, which can begin as early as preschool, accounts for 70 percent of reported bullying and is often a stepping stone to other types of aggression, including physical, relational, and online bullying. Hurtful words, both spoken and written, chip away at a child's budding sense of self, leaving fear, shame, and self-doubt in its place. As caring adults, how can we help children feel safe, respected, and confident in who they are?

We can start by holding children who bully others accountable for their behavior, while modeling and encouraging positive choices. We can help bystanders explore safe and effective ways to stand up for those who are being bullied. And through books such as *Weird!,* we can help kids like Luisa, who are targets of bullying, understand how to ask for help and how the words they say to themselves—their "self-talk"—can counteract hurtful words from others. Simple changes in the way kids think and act can have a positive impact on their self-confidence and influence bullying outcomes.

Reflection Questions for *Weird!*

The story told in *Weird!* illustrates a fictional situation, but it is one that many kids will likely relate to even if their experiences have been different. Following are some questions and activities to encourage reflection and dialogue as you read *Weird!* Referring to the main characters by name will help children make connections: *Luisa* is the target of the bullying, *Jayla* is a bystander to the bullying, and *Sam* initiates the bullying.

Important: **Online bullying (called *cyberbullying*) is a real threat among elementary-age children, given the increased use of smartphones and computers in school and at home. It's also the most difficult type of bullying to stop, because it's less apparent to onlookers. Be sure to include cyberbullying in all of your discussions about bullying with kids.**

Page 1: How do you think Luisa is feeling? Why do you think she feels that way?

Pages 2–11: What does Luisa do after Sam (the girl in her class) calls her "weird"? Why do you think she does that? Who are the other characters in the story? What are they doing as Sam bullies Luisa? What would you do if you saw someone being treated that way?

Pages 12–13: Luisa says, "It seems like *weird* is the only word she knows, and I don't know any words." What do you think she means?

Pages 14–15: Does Luisa look different on page 14? Why? Who are the characters on these two pages and why are they important?

Pages 16–17: Is it hard for Luisa to ask for help? Why? Who can you go to for help if you are being bullied? (**Note:** *Many kids suffer in silence when they are bullied, because they don't know who to ask for help or what to say. They might even think they deserve the bullying, worry that others won't believe them, assume they will get in trouble, or fear retaliation by the person doing the bullying. Assure kids that, while it may be difficult, it's important to ask for help—and to ask as many times as it takes to end the bullying.*)

Pages 18–19: What is Jayla (the girl in the background) doing with Luisa's boots on page 18? Why? What is Luisa doing with all the negative thoughts she wrote down before, and why?

> *Note:* **The activity on page 36 tells kids how to recycle negative thoughts into positive thoughts. This can be a complex process, so be sure to guide them through the steps.**

Pages 20–21: What are the other characters in the hallway doing and saying? How do you think that makes Luisa feel? How do you think that makes Sam feel?

Pages 22–25: What is different about Luisa on these pages? What is different about Sam? Why do you think Sam bullies? Why might other kids bully? Why is it wrong to bully?

Pages 26–31: What does Luisa discover? What are some things you can do to feel and look more confident? Let's rehearse them!

Overall: Which character in *Weird!* is most like you and why? What would you like to say to this character?

The Weird Series

The Weird series gives readers the opportunity to explore three very different perspectives on bullying: that of a child who is a target of bullying in *Weird!*, that of a bystander to bullying in *Dare!*, and that of a child who initiates bullying in *Tough!* Each book can be used alone or together with the other books in the series to build awareness and engage children in discussions related to bullying and encourage bullying prevention. If you are using the books as a series, consider doing the following activities with young readers.

Series Activity: Everyone Has a Role to Play

Discuss with children how we all have a role to play when it comes to ending bullying. Consider how it was easier for Luisa to start being herself again with the support from her family, her teachers, her classmates, and her friends. In small groups or as a class, role-play Luisa's story.

Series Activity: Memorable Moments

Have children fold a sheet of paper into three equal parts and label each part with one of the three book titles: *Weird!*, *Dare!*, and *Tough!* Invite children to draw what they think was the most important moment from each book in the corresponding section of the paper. Have children share their drawings and explain why they were memorable moments.

Series Activity: Circle of Courage

Ask children to consider specific acts of courage by others that made a difference for Luisa, Jayla, and Sam. Mount a large paper circle onto a bulletin board and write "Circle of Courage" in the center. Place a container with colorful paper polka dots, stars, and hearts next to the circle. Encourage children to add shapes to the circle whenever they witness an act of courage that helps prevent or stop bullying.

Series Activity: What Comes Next?

Weird! Dare! Tough! . . . what comes next? Ask children to imagine and make predictions about what happens to the characters in the next book. Encourage them to consider the main characters: *Luisa, Jayla,* and *Sam,* as well as the peripheral characters in the books: *Emily, Thomas, Patrick, Will, Mr. C.,* and *Alex.* Then have kids create and present their own book title and storyboard.

About the Author and Illustrator

Erin Frankel has a master's degree in English education and is passionate about teaching and writing. She taught ESL in Alabama before moving to Madrid, Spain, with her husband Alvaro and their three daughters, Gabriela, Sofia, and Kelsey. Erin knows firsthand what it feels like to be bullied, and she hopes her stories will help bring smiles back to children who have been involved in bullying. She and her longtime friend and illustrator Paula Heaphy share the belief that all children have the right to feel safe, loved, and confident in who they are. In her free time, Erin loves hiking in the Spanish mountains with her puppy Bella, as well as kayaking in her hometown of Mays Landing, New Jersey, which she visits as often as she can.

Paula Heaphy is a print and pattern designer in the fashion industry. She's an explorer of all artistic mediums from glassblowing to shoemaking, but her biggest love is drawing. She jumped at the chance to illustrate her friend Erin's story, having been bullied herself as a child. As the character of Luisa came to life on paper, Paula felt her path in life suddenly shift into focus. She lives in Brooklyn, New York, where she hopes to use her creativity to light up the hearts of children for years to come.

The Weird Series

by Erin Frankel, illustrated by Paula Heaphy. 48 pp. Ages 5–9.

More Great Books from Free Spirit

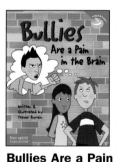
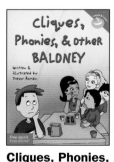

Bystander Power
by Phyllis Kaufman Goodstein and Elizabeth Verdick, illustrated by Steve Mark
128 pp. Ages 8–13.

Bullies Are a Pain in the Brain
written and illustrated by Trevor Romain
112 pp. Ages 8–13.

Cliques, Phonies, & Other Baloney
written and illustrated by Trevor Romain
136 pp. Ages 8–13.

Good-Bye Bully Machine
by Debbie Fox and Allan L. Beane, Ph.D., illustrated by Debbie Fox
48 pp. Ages 8 & up.

Interested in purchasing multiple quantities? Contact edsales@freespirit.com or call 1.800.735.7323 and ask for Education Sales.

Many Free Spirit authors are available for speaking engagements, workshops, and keynotes. Contact speakers@freespirit.com or call 1.800.735.7323.

For pricing information, to place an order, or to request a free catalog, contact:

free spirit PUBLISHING®

217 Fifth Avenue North • Suite 200 • Minneapolis, MN 55401-1299 • toll-free 800.735.7323 • local 612.338.2068
fax 612.337.5050 • help4kids@freespirit.com • www.freespirit.com